Dedalus Euro Shorts
General Editor: Timothy Lan

Ink in the Blood

Stéphanie Hochet

INK IN THE BLOOD

Translated by Mike Mitchell

Dedalus

Dedalus would like to thank the French Ministry of Culture in Paris for its assistance in producing this book and Arts Council, England for its support of the Dedalus publishing programme.

Supported using public funding by
ARTS COUNCIL
ENGLAND

Published in the UK by Dedalus Limited,
24-26, St Judith's Lane, Sawtry, Cambs, PE28 5XE
email: info@dedalusbooks.com
www.dedalusbooks.com

ISBN printed book 978 1 910213 11 7
ISBN ebook 978 1 910213 31 5

Dedalus is distributed in the USA & Canada by SCB Distributors
15608 South New Century Drive, Gardena, CA 90248
email: info@scbdistributors.com web: www.scbdistributors.com

Dedalus is distributed in Australia by Peribo Pty Ltd
58, Beaumont Road, Mount Kuring-gai, N.S.W. 2080
email: info@peribo.com.au

First published by Dedalus in 2015

Printed in Finland by Bookwell
Typeset by Marie Lane

Parker would be satisfied with each tattoo about a month, then something about it that had attracted him fell off.

'Parker's Back', Flannery O'Connor

Fads and fashions: a tribal bracelet, stars, surnames (Beckham, Scarface, Soprano…)

Chinese characters on your neck – avoid the neck if it's your first time.

Guns: *liner, shader, magnum*. A noisy or a silent machine. Ink. The quality of the blacks. Pure pigments, dense black, its scarcity justifying the price. Ink capsules. Gloves. Dettol, alcohol. Cellophane.

On your stomach, feeling like being sick.

Your ribs are so sensitive you can't think. Ankle, collarbone, solar plexus, elbows and armpits: unforgettable pain. The feeling that a fingernail is scratching you, *slowly*. The burning sensation brings to mind a well-known, stainless-steel instrument with a precise cutting edge: the scalpel… The most painful part is *filling in*, colouring the space between two lines dot by dot. It is advisable not to have it done on an empty stomach.

I'd never stopped thinking about it. For twenty years at least. The temptation had grown stronger with the years. The taboo surrounding it had not lessened its attraction, on the contrary. Without this taboo on the part of the family I would have given up the idea fairly quickly and turned to something else. It wouldn't have been worth wasting my time over it. The taboo gave substance to the fantasy.

At fifteen I was thinking of totemic emblems, wolf jaws, clan symbols. I dreamt of being the leader of a gang, of a political party. Ideologies gave me a thrill: power, yes, that was what it was about. At that time I felt totally detached from everything. That year I'd been in hospital with a serious illness. Shut up in a room for months on end, my thoughts just went round and round inside my head. That was when I started drawing. The pages in my notebooks were covered with weapons, crosses. Crosses that weren't Christian symbols.

I got better, I was no longer the boy obsessed with the idea of being a leader, with war and theories claiming to justify it. Getting better was not just a physical matter.

I turned my back on the thrill of conflict but I retained my taste for crosses and tattoos. It is a taste I will never lose. If one can ever say *never*.

I was sure that one day I would give in. It would have the symbolic force of military service, losing your virginity, marriage and death. In certain civilisations being given a tattoo is a rite of passage for young people reaching adulthood. Being behind schedule with my biological clock, I had not yet come to a final decision. Have it done, yes, but that still left the where, when, by whom and, above all, *what*. I surveyed those I saw on other people. Theirs looked botched to me, ludicrous. Had these people given serious thought to the meaning, to what it made them look like? Had they decided on the spur of the moment? Had they been disappointed when it was done? Those aren't the kind of questions you can ask openly but I thought about them all the same. In their place I wouldn't have put that star there and, anyway, I wouldn't have drawn it like that. Time to think about drawing.

Drawing opens up your mind. You think you know shapes, but no, you don't. The line draws you towards something you hadn't thought of, that is, you had been thinking: *something along the lines of that*, but once you get there it's a rather different *that* from what you had in mind. That's the surprise. The difficulty too. How to capture the trailing tentacles of the jellyfish, the wind in the blossoming cherry tree, the glassy sheen on the barrel of a gun, the flakes of black on a Bhutan's dagger? (Love precision.) A difficulty that's even greater if you intend to put the drawing onto a body. Remember the artists of the Lascaux caves who knew how to exploit the contours and curves of the walls, including them in their drawings, for example making a bulge in the rock represent an animal's hump. Play with what nature has given you. Practise on a flat sheet of paper, in the knowledge that nothing is flat on the human body. The body abhors flatness. Which part should you choose? Your side, your arm (the eternal tradition of sailors), your neck? Know that the elbow, the solar plexus, the soles of the feet, the palm of the hand must always be avoided. Apart from that everything is *tattooable. Tattooable?* So what should you choose? What meaning should you give to the part of your body you've selected? And feel like God in designating the spot the needle is going to pierce, for it is God alone who singles out which limb will suffer in an illness or in an accident in which bones will be broken.

Tattoos tell you about the world, about men's beliefs. The Greeks and Romans used to tattoo their slaves. With an owl for the Greek thralls whilst the Romans preferred to place the first letter of the master's surname between the slave's eyes… The man found in the Alps whose mummified body showed that he lived in the year 4,546 before Christ, the one they called Ötzi, was also tattooed. From the Picts in Scotland and right across Asia to the Aborigines in Australia people pierced their skin in order to inject pigment into it or – what was equally a sign of its importance – found this marking of the skin offensive (tattooing was forbidden by Judaism: 'Ye shall not make any cuttings in your flesh for the dead, nor print any marks upon you: I am the Lord.' Leviticus, ch. 19, v. 28). And what about the mark of Cain? Is that not the ultimate tattoo? The mark that follows you, that gives you away for ever. Tattoos are the most important of the distinguishing marks that are of interest to the police: it wasn't that long ago that such an adornment would only be worn by a man who was a *bad lot*, a man with a murky past and nefarious intentions. Can one imagine Jean Genet's Querelle without an anchor tattoo? Every detail of tattoos was noted down on index cards and used to identify criminals.

Roses blown apart by a bullet from a gun, an Indian goddess with arms stretched out in a lascivious dance, a Rottweiler tearing its owner's shoulder to pieces, a clown, a juggling monkey, a ship's prow emerging from the flesh, a spider with a human face puffing at a Lucky Strike, a bear, a lone wolf, from Kazakhstan or Tasmania, a pin-up, I-love-you-Mum, forever-yours-Lola, nobody's-perfect, etc. And then the crosses, all kinds of crosses: Latin, Greek, Papal, Celtic or Egyptian. Hundreds throughout the world. Esotericism, spiritualism, a symbol: religious, military, political. Poetic.

I'll know more about you when I've seen: What image, what phrase do you have profaning your skin? What could be worth lasting as long as your body, of decaying along with you?

I went to several studios looking for a tattoo artist who would be willing to talk to me in detail about his work. I wandered round the 9th, 10th and 11th arrondissements in Paris. They weren't friendly, weren't chatty, there was something not quite right about them. I wasn't interested in some loutish ex-sailor who'd settled down with a well-established studio and works crudely. If he presses too hard, draws badly, economises on materials, I turn away. I'll call back another time, I say for the sake of politeness.

Then I met Dimitri.

Spring

I set off for Italy, for Turin. I'm going in order to explore the Po valley. Claudio, a friend, puts me up in his city-centre apartment above the arcades. Big rooms, high ceilings, friezes on the walls. Middle-class families used to live here in prosperous days. Today these rooms house an intellectual couple. Claudio teaches Latin at the university, writes erudite and polished novels that carry the reader off into the Middle Ages. His partner, Marilisa, is an art critic.

It's hot. Summer is a little ahead of schedule, has settled down among the hills; there's a heaviness in the air. We only go out into the town towards the end of the afternoon. Seeing the churches again, the cafés, the squares, the tiny shops where you chat with the owner. We stroll.

The next day it's Marilisa who's driving the little Fiat. Claudio doesn't like cars. He's wary of speed and of the aggressiveness of people at the wheel. He's too bound up in his contemplative nature to drive. Several hours in the car. I've plenty of time to think about the aerial photographs of the Po delta again. A succession of sandbanks, aluminium clouds, the deep blue of the Adriatic, the Po meandering towards the salt water when a part of it (its river subconscious) is seized with a vague desire for independence and branches off to make its own way to the mouth. We walk along the banks. The dreamy banks. Devastated during floods by the unpredictable water. Land raped by the river, it makes you think of the rape of Lucretia. Thoughts of old Italy, of the land, formerly under water, on which we're walking. Of the Etruscans and the Romans. As we're walking Claudio takes my arm: You wouldn't like to go to the Museum of Antiquities, would you? Claudio and Marilisa hold culture in high regard and also particularly enjoy admiring it in enclosed spaces.

Yes, what a good idea. Marilisa looks at her watch. In that case we'd better hurry up.

Museum

As it's the Easter holidays my friends have some time to spare. We drove on as far as Genoa. Coins with the effigy of Ptolemy XIII Philocrator, jars, red earthenware dishes, mosaics with graffiti of the names of popular gladiators scrawled on them. Wonderful and familiar objects. Suddenly, in a glass case, a plaque. A sundial of absolute simplicity with its austere style and superfluous Roman numerals, insect-black on the yellow stone, the hours waiting for the shadow of the gnomon to fall on them, time standing still.

An inscription. In small letters, true, but legible: *vulnerant omnes, ultima necat*. As I was hopeless at Latin at school and have never tried to do anything about it, I asked Claudio for a translation.

They all wound, the last one kills.

I repeat the Latin phrase. Out loud at first.

It's about the hours, Claudio says.

I can't explain the surprise and emotion this sentence arouses in me. I say nothing, I'm storing up something or other. Agitation, dizziness – *hours*, that's it exactly. I can't tear myself away from the display case in which, standing on a little piece of plastic, is the sundial.

I don't have a fetish about watches, I don't wear one. A girlfriend gave me one with her family coat of arms engraved on it… When the watch stopped, I saw it as a sign. Our time was over. We split up a few weeks later, without any need of explanation. That's life. It meant I avoided getting married. Marriage? I had sensed it coming, that insidious union only death can dissolve. Happiness decreed by contract.

This phrase is often found on the Romans' sundials, Claudio tells me. From their need to have a *memento mori* on the objects that served as clocks. Who would dare write it on their Swatch nowadays? Nowadays no one wants to think of death.

We continue to go round the Genoa museum. But I'm tired. Marilisa makes a respectful pause before each work of art, each everyday object from the Roman period, absorbed in reading the explanatory labels. Here ladies' toilet articles, combs, mirrors, farther on toys, little carved horses, bears… Seeing what the earth has spewed up, I imagine things the digs have not yet revealed, traces of human life still macerating in the entrails of the ground. Remains of the Etruscans and Romans. If we dig deeper, encounters with Cro-Magnons, Neanderthals… difficult to restrain our fantasies about ancestors. We'd like to see them come alive again, performing *danses macabres* several metres under the ground.

Back in Turin, in Claudio and Marilisa's apartment, I write the adage down on a sheet of paper. Such concise and compact formulations are rare. Everything is there. Its beauty strikes me like a perfect object. It could be a Ming vase or a statuette from ancient Egypt. It's a sentence. An example of chiasmus, Claudio explains. A stylistic device in which the words form a cross.

Claudio has just said the word 'cross'. I'm dumbfounded. It's not just the meaning of the sentence, it's the form as well that makes it so appealing. I turn the sheet over and write it down in the form of a cross, the second phrase as a vertical line straddling the first. Claudio examines the words that look like a calligram. Smiles. Yes, he says softly, that's it exactly. For a moment we gaze dreamily at the sentence that's become a design. An enigma.

Marilisa asks whether it's common to have sentences as tattoos.

Yes, it's a fashion that's come in recently. *That which doesn't kill me, makes me stronger* has been a great hit, Nietzsche has become trendy. In America, especially among gang members or those who'd like to be one, you can often see *Only God can judge me*, verbal arrogance typical of a hooligan. The problem, I tell Marilisa, is that a tattoo like that is only original for the one who sets off the vogue. When it's imitated it becomes ridiculous, an adolescent slogan. What is the point of pressing your own body into service if everyone can see themselves in what you've had tattooed on it?

I often talk about the profession with Marilisa and Claudio. They know that I show designs to a tattoo artist, that I'm fascinated by tattooing. Even if I haven't yet yielded to the temptation to offer up my own skin.

Tattooing

Dimitri's more than a professional, he's an artist. He works with a state-of-the-art, silent rotary machine. Some people claim to have felt virtually nothing while he was tattooing them. This miracle is all down to him, to his marvellous technique, to his delicate touch. In the Paris tattoo scene Dimitri rules, everyone involved in it knows him.

Broad and tall, his head smooth-shaved, bulging flesh on the back of his neck, it would be pointless (crazy) to pick a quarrel with him. In more bloodthirsty times he would have been an executioner or a butcher. His bearing, his body speak for themselves. No trace of emotion or madness in his look, nor of malice either. The man's intimidating and reassuring at the same time. If he wasn't a tattoo artist, he'd surely make a good masseur: working with his hands on bodies. You can imagine the size of his muscles. He inspires a confidence that is close to plain submission.

Without him I would know nothing about tattooing. I watched him at work. He encouraged me to practise with a liner on pieces of fake skin, strange imitations you practise on to get your hand in. I took them and kneaded them, fascinated. Impossible not to think of the lampshades made of human skin in the Nazi extermination camps. Or of medical plates of figures with their limbs opened up and stripped of the skin.

Dimitri liked my designs. He draws pretty well himself, he has a sure hand, inventive. But I suggested some different kinds of imagery: people from the Middle Ages mounted on dragons, mythical monsters under the stars, cabbalistic signs. They brought a touch of the esoteric to his collection.

One day he said to me: You can tattoo me if you want to train yourself on real skin. But I didn't dare. I found it disturbing: the offer, the immediate opportunity, his acceptance of the intrusion on his body. It frightened me. I saw it as a proposition comparable to a sexual advance. Like: You can have me, you know.

His body is covered in strange figures, symbols, all kinds of cosmic tattoos. Some designs are the fruit of my imagination but it was he who injected the ink into his skin. Several times I watched him tattooing his thigh, his legs. This doesn't cause him any problems, on the contrary he prefers it that way, it's less painful when you're working on your own skin yourself, he says. I admired his calmness, his meticulous concentration, his big hands stretching his skin. He rubbed himself down with some kitchen roll and it started to go red; the colours of the tattoo were as intense as patches of blood.

I bring some new sketches back from Italy with me. Drawings of coins from the Roman period, some fine emperors' heads engraved on gold, faces with more savage expressions, shaggy hair, staring eyes. I like their air of mystery.

Eleven o'clock, Dimitri has just opened his studio. I haven't seen him for two weeks, I've missed him. We embrace. I'm dumbfounded by the strength and warmth of his hand on the nape of my neck, I feel like a kitten grabbed by the neck: benumbed and trusting. You look good, he says. I've brought you some drawings, made in Italy. My hands trembling with excitement, I open my portfolio.

Put them there, on the table.

The table = his desk where there's a mishmash of paper, syringes, bottles of alcohol, a roll of cellophane, latex gloves. I manage to find a space for my designs. Dimitri looks at the drawings in silence, scrutinising every detail. He picks up the sheets, one after the other, his big, virile body emitting a *Hmm* at each one. He pauses over the last. Reads out loud, *Vulnerant omnes, ultima necat*. Oh yes, he says, those Latin sundials. It's not bad, not bad at all, that one. He taps the sentence with the knuckle of his index finger.

A One-off

Is it to be Dimitri or me?

I've been asking myself that question all night. I had the choice. My hand wouldn't be sure, I'd be clumsy, just imagine the trembling, the mistakes, the nightmare. For a first tattoo it has to be him. Him who tattoos me. That's what I proposed to Dimitri. OK, he said with no show of emotion. Where d'you want it? On my *solar* plexus, I said.

He smiled, well aware of the connection between a sundial and the solar plexus.

It'll hurt, he said softly.

I know.

I know, but no one can imagine what you'll feel as long as you've not had it done. Dimitri smears alcohol over the part of my chest that I shaved that morning. Then he positions the tracing paper on which he's reproduced my design, the words arranged in a cross. The ink appears on my skin.

So now I'm in his hands. Forsaken, like a prisoner put to the *question* by his torturer. Relax, Dimitri advises. He's noticed I'm breathing quickly. He's going to take his time, allay my misgivings before getting down to work.

The solar plexus is an important network of nerves controlling all the main organs of the abdomen. The liver, the pancreas, the spleen and the kidneys are linked up to it. A violent shock to that area can send a man into a coma.

I knew all that but I'd made up my mind.

The pain is such a horror that you learn nothing from it, on the contrary it could make you turn stupid and nasty. After five minutes I wish I hadn't started. I come close to fainting, spewing up, slapping Dimitri. I'd like to give up the whole idea, but it's too late.

After twenty minutes my body has released endorphins and the pain is almost bearable. Relative anaesthesia. Dimitri works on my skin for another hour. Meticulous, he doesn't omit a single detail of the upstrokes and downstrokes of each letter, exerts just as much pressure as is necessary. The noise of the machine is forgotten, no longer gets on my nerves, is like the sound of an electric razor. I observe the eyebrows, the features of this man in whom I've put my trust, there's no doubt that his calmness is more effective than the natural anaesthetic my body secretes. I'm hanging on the expression of his lips, his eyes, I listen to the rhythm of his breathing as if my life itself depended on this man's gestures, his good will. Then I close my eyes and recite prayers of the Mahatma, Sanskrit incantations or some I invent in a language of my own with Indian sounds.

One last rub over my skin with kitchen towel. Dimitri leaves me without a word, I hear his footsteps moving away across the room. I keep my eyes closed. He pours himself a glass of water from the tap, offers me one. I become aware that I'm thirsty, my mouth feels like pasteboard. I sit up to take the glass, have a look at the tattoo.

It's magnificent.

The cross looks as if it has grown on my solar plexus of its own accord. It highlights my torso, recalls the pattern on the abdomen of certain rare butterflies. When I'm in motion, it moves with me; however, if you look closely, its movement seems to continue on its own when I'm still. You could believe the cross is alive, you expect it to turn on its axis and free itself from the supporting epidermis. The letters are dazzling, the words stick out as if in relief.

A quick glance would record it simply as a cross. I have an odd sense of being branded like a cow or bull, at the same time feeling set apart, protected by this talismanic sign. Like one of the faithful a priest has blessed.

The irritation on my skin has gone and there's no swelling.

During the day my clothes hide that which, from now on, I call my *Vulnerant*.

I'm still the same man. Am I the same man? Not exactly, there's something else inside me, something that is close to my heart – so close that I was happy to suffer so that it would belong to me or mark me out or bring me luck or quite the opposite. I quickly told myself that these words were mine alone. As I became aware of the way my skin was absorbing the meaning, the questioning began.

Do these words have the same meaning now that they have been inserted between the dermis and the epidermis? On a sundial *they all wound, the last one kills*, refers to the hours. In Latin an hour – *hora* – is a feminine noun, as in French. But without the sundial what is the identity of that noun?

Mulieres

I've known lots of women but I've seldom formed an attachment. I've known lots of women *because* I've seldom formed an attachment or I've seldom formed an attachment *because* I've known lots of women, I'm not sure which. My relations with them have been like a domino effect, each piece, as it falls, taking the next one down with it. I have never become emotionally involved in a relationship, it's beyond me, I'm not capable of it, I don't want it. Women like me, I've always appealed to women but I don't take any particular pride in it. I don't know, perhaps I should have thought about it, questioned my own lack of maturity, my psychological stability.

I love women like sisters, without any desire to possess them for life, simply desiring them during the act of love. I'm often glad when they break with me. I'm reluctant to hurt them and breaking with them hurts them.

I keep Dimitri up to date on the Christian name of the woman I happen to be going round with for a few days, sometimes a few weeks. He's amazed at my fickleness. He remains steadfastly unattached. I don't know the reason for his celibacy, if I were a woman, I'd want Dimitri. He's tall, strong, reassuring. His voice envelops you in its masculine warmth. It must be nice for a woman to hear that voice whispering sweet nothings, cajoling you with men's words. An invitation to let yourself go. Its resonant tone evokes the embrace of strong arms. But perhaps I know nothing about women's tastes, that's quite likely.

Adorned with my *Vulnerant*, I can't resist the pleasure of showing it off. But not just anyhow, not just to anybody and everybody. Only in private, only to the women I've seduced, in the way you reveal a secret part of yourself. Oh, my impatience to see their reaction of surprise and admiration that I'm already imagining. To hear their remarks or questions, no matter whether they're stupid or astute. People are never indifferent to these kinds of marks on the body. Everyone has something to say about them. I'm sure that for some people hearing others' opinion is an end in itself, the very reason for their tattoo. For me it's something different, but what? I've all the time in the world to find out. But there's one clue: only show it to those *women*.

I need to get to know it better. Need someone else seeing it to make it more truly my own. Need the question: Is that Latin? And then: What does it mean? Oh, the pleasure of confirming and explaining, forefinger on my chest, reading the tattoo as a boy follows the words of the Torah during his bar-mitzvah. Writing, the word of the divinity, writing in a love affair, writing and life.

I have to admit that I can't make up my mind what kind of woman I should display my *Vulnerant* to. Maturity is a valued characteristic of men – at least that's what people say to flatter us – but I'm clear enough about myself to know that I have the same expectations as in my younger days. She has to be at least a little bit pretty.

She's called Sandrine. She reminds me of a friend at school. Slim, shy, her figure emphasised by a tight-waisted skai dress. She's young, 25 – I could be her father but I wouldn't want to be. Works at a till in a supermarket. A slightly drowsy look, a smile both apologetic and timid. She's rather like a sparrow or a tiny rodent, a furtive animal, a bit scatterbrained, though less scatterbrained than apprehensive, on the alert. Since supermarkets always get me down – you meet any number of frumpish women and coarse people there – I'm grateful to this young woman for embodying the terror and swiftness of rodents, a living representation. When I come to pay for my shopping, I rummage round feverishly in my pockets for some loose change, make a joke about it. She finds my confusion, my comical gestures amusing. She smiles. I quickly look for something to say, I get into gear, I keep going, I don't let any awkwardness arise. I suggest we meet, *to have a chat*, I add.

I invite her out for a meal – furtive animals are often famished. I invite her back for a drink. I invite her to get undressed.

In the morning she sees it. She looks. My *Vulnerant* is scrutinised, touched. Not a single word comes from the creature's lips. Amazement. My amazement. Why does she not ask any questions? Does this young woman understand Latin? I wouldn't have thought so. I have to admit I'm disappointed. Not a word.

My joy at the moment of parting. Slightly tense and solemn, Sandrine, asks, 'You can say so if you don't want to, but…' A rush of hope. At last! She's going to ask about the Latin phrase. My heart starts to pound, isn't it marvellous of her to wait for the moment of parting to pluck up the courage, and how timidly, like a little kid, squirming, uneasy at addressing an adult. My soft spot for childlike women. '…would you like to have my telephone number?' Hope fades. Leaving nothing but a white lie: 'Yes, of course I want your number.' What a disappointment!

I don't call Sandrine. Cross off Sandrine.

I work my socks off. My illustrations for the press bring in a bit of money. When I've a free moment I make more and more designs. Especially for Dimitri.

A twinge of regret when I think of Sandrine. It's the first time I've been disturbed by my relationship with a woman. None has previously made me suffer. A strange feeling: I thought I was going to have a cursory affair but our parting showed that I had wrongly interpreted our relationship. I start seeing Sandrine's face in my dreams. And always the question: why did she not comment on my tattoo?

There's plenty more fish in the sea, etc. Stick to popular sayings. She's called Jeanne. She's studying Sociology at Nanterre. She shares a flat with a freelance journalist I know. A student atmosphere, Nanterre, it almost takes you back to May '68. Jeanne has translucent skin, an elongated face, she's as beautiful as a virgin by Van Eyck. Her nose is pierced, the ring she wears in it makes me want to call her my little bull ('The Little Bull who was a Van Eyck Virgin' – has any writer ever thought of that as the title for a novel?). I restrain myself. We go to a bar, the three of us, my freelance friend, Jeanne and me. Jeanne spends the evening teasing me, taunting me, prodding me playfully with her shoulders, elbows, knees. I say silly things, I'm provoking, challenging. We give each other questioning looks, we respond, everything's simple. After the bar, we end up in her room. And I get undressed. She looks, open-mouthed. Fantastic, your tattoo, but… She breaks off, comes over to have a better look.

Is it normal for the first letters to be less legible than the rest? Her question has a chilling effect on me. I look at my chest, rush into the bathroom. Refusing to believe this, I lean towards the mirror. The first part of the saying is, indeed, lighter. It's faint but still visible. Beginning to fade. It's worrying. I can't sleep for thinking about it.

Jeanne, Jeanne, Jeanne. I merely have to say her name to be overcome with humiliation. I associate Jeanne with the beginning of the deterioration of my tattoo, with the taste of defeat. Is my *Vulnerant* making me less strong? The feeling of humiliation intensifies, saps my strength and I wake up every night following that evening bathed, almost half drowning, in sweat.

Part of the inscription is getting progressively fainter. It's as if the ink of the first words is being diluted, is escaping somewhere, into some unknown area of my anatomy. I check every morning in the mirror. The black is fading, but so slowly that at first I didn't notice. What is strange, or at least *remarkable*, is the discrepancy in the colours between the first and last words. It's as if a piece of tracing paper had been placed over the words *Vulnerant omnes* and its opacity is changing the appearance of the colours. Every day it gets worse. I hesitate to talk to Dimitri about it. I'm sure he's never come across a case like this before. He would have mentioned it. He uses quality ink and knows his job, I've never met anyone so professional; that last statement goes round and round in my head, goes with me everywhere. As for myself, I haven't had a bath since the tattoo was done in order to avoid my pores opening and allowing the pigment to escape. I have no explanation for it. Full of concern, I scrutinise my chest then stop thinking about it. At least I *try* to stop thinking about it.

I have a strange feeling while I'm half asleep that my hand is feeling the place where my tattoo is and a restless subliminal thought surfaces again. The next morning I take a shower without looking at *the place* and slip into a room with no mirror where I can dry myself in peace.

I spend the following days behaving as if I wasn't thinking about it, taking the kind of precautions to avoid it you would use so as not to disturb a predator in the jungle. But if I'm in some public place I have the impression that people – more numerous than *before* – are watching me. And their eyes seem to linger over that part of my anatomy, as if my clothes couldn't hide it entirely.

Suddenly it's a frenzy of encounters. For some vague reason I feel like taking my clothes off, being naked again, so as to convince myself there's nothing abnormal about me. Neither about my body nor my tattoo. I'm 45. It's what people would call an urge for sex provoked by a midlife crisis.

It's a rather merry and slightly stupid period when all my outfits seem to itch and I can't wait to get out of them as fast as I can, to soothe the itch, to feel as much fresh air round me as possible. It's summer, it's Cesare Pavese's *time when every day was a holiday*, my youth has come back for a while, just a hint perhaps, as long as the delusion lasts. Even delusions can give you strength.

I'd like to be light-hearted, leave worrying behind and frolic, forgetting my age. So far I've looked after my body. I haven't accumulated the fat round the stomach muscles that's a threat to every man over 25. Sport helped, as has my self-critical narcissism. I make the most of that by going to the swimming pool, the sauna. Working on my drawings at night frees up hours during the day. Coming out of one pool I attract the attention of a gang of children. These cherubic little hooligans nudge each other with their shoulders, pointing at me with their chins. One of the boys turns round, concealing an incipient laugh with his hand; it's as if he were grasping his snide remark in his palm, clutching his glee like a handful of dust. *Hey, clock that!* The little brats are laughing fit to burst. At first I don't understand, then I realise what they're pointing at. My *Vulnerant* setting off an outburst of uproarious laughter! I don't know where to look. Get dressed as quickly as possible and, above all, don't let on how upset I am.

At their age I was no better. It's a violent reminder of the reality of my tattoo, of the cruelty of young people. All I want to do is to get away from the swimming pool and go home with my tail between my legs. However: don't let it get you down. Tell yourself you have to go out and face the world again, recover your pride and wait for the evening.

I could make believe that I have money and thus win other people over, spend, spend, spend. I can wear a well-tailored suit and make it look a million dollars, it's all a matter of creating an illusion. Add to that a pleasant smile, a smooth voice and – important – manicured fingernails. I'm in a smart café, I buy drinks for women I find attractive. I sometimes lie about my work: lawyer, doctor, professor. Or a film director (I change my nationality with a preference for the Baltic states), a critic on *Télérama*. I mention a well-known name and pretend it's my pseudonym, I'm an artist etc. I make them laugh, sometimes. I get given telephone numbers. I'm a completely different person, at ease, with a ready tongue, charming. Some encounters lead to intercourse, which is all I'm looking for. There's nothing else to say about them except that these occasions allow me to bare my torso.

Baring my torso becomes an obsession. How many times can I bare my torso?

Could my tattoo have become the most interesting part of my body as I present it to the opposite sex? Assuming a woman likes this *Vulnerant*, can understand it. If only one of them could see what it is: my innermost self, the most intimate part of my being. So far none has really appreciated its significance, its philosophical depth. It's as if women pass me by, as if I were a man just like the rest. Nothing remains of those nights. I ought to just shrug my shoulders, forget these humiliations. After several experiences of this kind, I become downhearted: no woman sees me the way I am, none can read the Latin sentence properly.

Conversation with Dimitri:

Him: You're still happy with your tattoo?

Me: Yes.

Him: Has it healed up well?

Me: Perfectly. No question.

Him (*roguishly*): Perhaps you're going to get hooked – and become one of my regulars.

Me: This one's enough for me.

Dimitri doesn't press the matter. I'm intrigued by the fact that he doesn't pursue it but it's quite right. After all, I like his discretion. In my view discretion is a male virtue, curiosity is considered feminine. And I like the fact that Dimitri doesn't parody women. So why do I have the impression he doesn't believe me? Am I starting to go through a paranoid phase? The question wearies me. I feel my forehead: I have a temperature.

It took me months to get to know Dimitri, months for him to open up to me. His childhood in a provincial town put him off the cramped little lives he observed. Brought up by a father who was a soldier, strict and narrow-minded, the first thing Dimitri learnt was to hold his tongue. He was the kind of pupil who, whatever the subject, spent his time in class doodling, drawing on scrap paper while the others were taking notes on the lesson. Intelligent enough to get satisfactory results at school without having to make an effort, he lived from day to day with his hatred of his father that finally kept him warm, just as a lice-ridden coat will keep a down-and-out warm. He left home at 17, joined the navy, and his parents lost sight of him for two years. His mother, who received just a handful of postcards – five in 24 months – imagines him on the Pacific Ocean, a tiny speck on a watery sphere putting in at islands the size of pinheads, savage as virgin forests, haunted by half-human, half-animal creatures forever lost to civilisation. Then she has a foreboding (her feminine intuition): he's on the Adriatic, sailing along the shores, the target of the seductive arts of Italian and Croatian women, as good as married or learning to play the mandolin. She fears he might cross the China Sea with its deadly dangerous rollers, the hypocrisy of those people is well known, also their cruelty: the originality they showed in devising tortures has been so widely reported they could have taken out a patent for it. Given her imagination she's never short of fantasies.

With no news of his son, Dimitri's father assumes he'll never return, loses no time in accepting the idea and starts converting his son's bedroom into a study where he can show his slides. He uses it as a store for his own belongings and hangs a portrait of himself on the wall. In it he's in uniform and standing to attention. It's a black-and-white photo taken during the *events* in Algeria, the kind of thing you might find in any family, except that Dimitri's father was a *regular* soldier, a career Dimitri thinks disgusting but doesn't avoid when, as an adolescent, he joins the navy. Proving you can copy things you detest. On the ships he gets to know sailors, he also gets to know tattoos. It's the same in the ports. At 18 he has a starfish tattooed on his shoulder. It's quite well done and later lotus flowers and waves come to keep it company. The tattoo artist is Chinese, (a Chinese from the Philippines, but still) which would worry his mother but attracts the young man. The ancient civilisation had perfected the art: clear lines, vivid motifs and the fine oriental imagination producing hydra-headed monsters and other fantastical creatures. Inevitably Dimitri becomes addicted. At the next port he has his thigh done – and there he is with a dragon spewing out flames onto his knee. Eventually Dimitri even comes to enjoy the pain on his skin: the little beast torturing you, slowly pecking away at your skin. Everything fascinates him, he follows the man's movements, studies him, asks questions, remembers. He knows what he will do after the navy. During those years he found his passion and it was his comfort and strength in his self-imposed silence. Some of the other sailors nicknamed him Mr Mum.

One morning I wake up with a temperature once again. A pool of sweat on the sheets. This has been happening more and more often. Even though I'm good at putting things I don't like out of my mind, my body isn't well and it's impossible to ignore it. A feeling of complete exhaustion can suddenly come over me at any time of the day. The room where I'm working shrinks, the furniture starts to move in a circle round me, then the movement becomes hesitant. I wait for it to stop, for order to be restored. Is it my own perception that has changed? I get up. Shower, shave then brush my teeth. My gums are bleeding.

I think of going to the doctor. I decide to go to the doctor. I go to the doctor. Just taking that decision exhausts me. I'm booked in for a blood test.

Marie. A name to make you dream. Marie, Marie, Marie. Three times. Always repeat the first name of a woman three times. Of a woman like that. Say, chant the incantation to the Virgin. Marie is such a beautiful name some men have taken it. Just as some men wear dresses – out of tradition or out of daring and sophistication. Lafayette, a manly hero, was called Marie. Marie Lafayette, the champion of liberty, the American idol. On a young and beautiful woman the name of Marie is an excess of purity, a virginal tautology, a crown of letters.

I meet Marie who's a lab assistant in a health centre. She appears clothed in a white coat on which is pinned a gilt badge with her first name. Her Titian-red hair is drawn back in a clip, a classic hairstyle that could be that of Eugénie Grandet or Anna Karenina. Lab assistants are beyond other women. Because of their dress. White coats look good on lab assistants, white coats look good to men.

Sitting in the chair designed for taking blood samples, I stretch out my arm. Watch her set about it: cotton wool, alcohol, applying the cuff on my biceps, all with an air of concentration and gentleness (the gentleness of her name). The pressure on my arm gives me a strange pleasure. Clench your fist. Breathe. Tender commands. The thick line of red trickles into the transparent tube. The calm flow of life, so beautiful to watch, so *calm*. The drip-by-drip of time. Does life slip by in the same way as the blood is flowing out? It pleases me to think so, and it pleases me even more to associate this efflux with the power over life and death of this young woman. How pleasant it is to abandon oneself, how sweet death would be in these conditions. No pain, no anguish. I would be trusting and the sight of this serene face would accompany me across to the other side. Numbness – oblivion – relief – letting go. The gentle pressure of my weakened body as it succumbs, resigns:

an offering. Its almost vegetable passivity would carry it to the very limit of being, smoothly, in a sensation of constant ecstasy. My body would grow heavy, then light, disconnected from its reality. Marie withdraws the needle. She takes it out just before it makes me faint. It's almost a pity. There, press firmly, she instructs me with a smile. The smile gives me hope.

I fall in love with Marie.

In love with Marie. I give this fact earnest consideration. I have no idea how to seduce a woman I'm in love with, the emotion is alien to me. The young woman seems even more inaccessible. I'm going to have to wait for the results of the test to declare my love.

But how?

I go and see Dimitri again. Not a word about my tattoo. The taboo between us is growing. He tells me that one of his clients is suffering from swelling and inflammation on an arm that's just been tattooed.

I've got nothing like that! I exclaim before he even asks. I show him my new designs and we have a beer together. There's a horizontal furrow across his forehead that I haven't seen before, as if he's worried. I say nothing. Questions bubbling up inside my head.

Back home I take my clothes off in front of the bathroom mirror. My torso, almost hairless, ought to be the best part of my body to have the *Vulnerant*. The idea was that the tattoo should disperse its symbolic power from the solar plexus to the most distant members. I stare, aghast. The first words: *Vulnerant omnes* are no longer legible, the ink under the epidermis has run leaving, as it spread, only a vague trace, the black gradually shading off with nothing that recalls the letters. All that can still be read is the second part of the epigram: *ultima necat.*

The shock.

I touch, I feel my skin. It hurts. In the not-so-distant past people removed tattoos with glasspaper. You rubbed them until they were inflamed, you tore off the skin. We are, thank God, no longer forced to rely on this barbaric method, the laser provides a solution. But what about my case? Am I visited during the night by a succubus that doesn't like my *Vulnerant* and uses its power to erase it? Does she claw at my chest while we're making love? I treat the inflammation with alcohol. I have the impression it's healing over.

I think about Marie. I think about her and the thought becomes unbearable. The more I think about her the more distant she becomes. An inaccessible object of desire. How can I get her to love me so that I can take her? I can't sleep, the prospect of getting nowhere with her would make me want to cry. I get up, dress and go out.

The long bank. The long bank illuminated by the boats berthed there garlanded with light. The retaining wall of the river with vegetation spewing over it.The music muffled by the closed bulkheads of the barges. You can go in. I've money in my pocket. Too much. To live above your means. It's a floating place where you can get a drink, where no one goes to bed before the morning. I'll have something to help me forget Marie.

Anna's Russian. As her name tells you, she says. Highly strung, skinny, red-haired, alcoholic – everything that people say about the Russians. Or that I see in her *a priori* because I know where she comes from. Is she doing it deliberately or am I just accepting received ideas? The barge is swaying slightly, though I only realise that after a few glasses. I'm hot, I'm sweating. Anna's hair is a fire calling to me: the attraction of danger. Anna leads me on, urges me to drink, partly out of defiance and, doubtless, partly out of calculation. But who could resist her etherial laughter. A wad of notes in my hand. Nothing lighter than those bits of paper, especially in Anna's company. She works in a circus. The way she pronounces circus is so charming I have to restrain myself not to kiss her. But no, eventually I don't restrain myself any longer. Her face touches mine. Was it she who came closer? Or me? Our teeth bite. Nibble at whatever they find in their path. I see the circus. Closing my eyes, I see Anna on a trapeze and I want to look away when she swings forward and lets go. A cloud of colours, red, white and black, trailing through the air in an elaborate swirl. A red summer night's dream. I suspect Anna's a bogus Russian (just as you can be a bogus redhead), an actress spinning out the exotic role with imitations. A girl paid to encourage men to drink. I find her even more moving. I become aware that I haven't any more money. My hand rummages round in my pocket: nothing. The feeling of metal in my mouth. I swallow. The same taste again. I spit in my handkerchief: a red blotch. My gums are on fire.

We abandon ship, leave the barge. My sea-legs are giving way. Anna helps me to walk; she herself has to lean on my arm just to put one foot in front of the other. We end up in a room somewhere.

I open one eye. When I try to turn over I find I'm stuck. My feet, my wrists are bound, it's painful. Neatly tied up in a strange room, I wonder what's happened, what's happening, what's going to happen. I've never been in such an awkward situation. Something else penetrates my consciousness: my whole body is inflamed, covered in streaks that sting, like a striped garment. I raise my head as much as I can: I'm naked and someone's scratched my chest, my back, my shoulders. It smarts so much it makes my eyes water.

I'm liberated by a cleaning woman. I leave the hotel, ashamed and penniless.

So ashamed that I don't mention the incident to anyone.

Dimitri

I like asking Dimitri about what's all the rage at the moment. I'm susceptible to the whorish aspect of fashion, the obscenity of the in-thing. It's my little weakness, my venial sin, my inglorious and inconsequential pastime, savouring the juicy morsels Dimitri is happy to throw me in return for… (for what?) for my gratitude. The honest pleasure I feel. I could leaf through fashion magazines, stuff for women or repressed queers, but the fashion I like is not an ephemeral confection in cloth, it's ink implanted under the skin for good. I meet my tattoo artist just as he's about to close his shop, his last client has just left, Dimitri's tidying his things away. He's rolled up his shirt sleeves. Marvellous to see again the lotus flowers between his wrist and biceps, the waves surging up to his shoulder. While the other arm is a harrowing counterpart: a man in an iron collar, inspired by a Goya sketch. The man being tortured has his mouth open, screaming, body twisted, grimacing, neck distorted by suffering. The lotus flowers and the waves are a souvenir from Manila, the Goya was created in Budapest – Dimitri has travelled around a lot, continuing to do so after he left the navy, for tattoos are done all over the world. He's very proud of his arms. He shows them off, maintains the musculature, daily exercises, press-ups etc. His old threadbare jeans are not particularly clean and there he is, dressed with a touch of the poetical, a hooligan style that says how virile, how male he is. His eyes blur, just a mist rising and dying away. Still with the worry line on his forehead. A smile. Just look at that mess, he says, jerking his chin in the direction of the back of his studio.

All the tracings with the most recent designs for tattoos are there. Crumpled corpses.

I don't know what it is about palaeontology that gets people but at the moment all I'm doing is fossils, trilobites and that kind of thing. That and portrayals of the Flood. The Bible and all that… I'm knackered. How are you?

I ought to talk about my tattoo. About the bit that's simply faded away leaving only *ultima necat* legible. About how I can't understand it. About Anna and her nails slashing my body, about Marie, whom I'm going to see in three days and whom I find disturbing, so disturbing it's enough to make me ill. Impossible to talk about it. I tell him I'm okay. He observes me in silence. I've always had the impression he has the ability to read me like a book. And not only me, I'm convinced he has power over people. It's the only way to explain his talent for his work. The sorcerer's art. Could Dimitri have been initiated into some taboo alchemy, some black art he keeps secret? I imagine him worming his way into people's thoughts just as he goes into their bodies, unhesitatingly and skilfully, inserting what he wants there without having to justify himself.

We have a beer in a café across the road from his studio. The heat's almost unbearable. Our clothes are sticking to our skin, the atmosphere in the city is highly charged, there's an argument going on just in front of us, perhaps they're going to come to blows – it's the Paris summer. I look up: the sky's full of angry clouds, the sky's in motion, like tattooed skin harassed by the spirits of the furious animals that have been drawn on it. The feeling that a murder is being prepared somewhere. Where? Nearby or a long way away, obviously, the thing has to take place somewhere or other. Those are my thoughts, my intuitions, completely involuntary of course. I dismiss these reflections. Dimitri has just lit a cigarette and has his gaze fixed on the end of his fag. Neither of us can think of anything to say but all at once I hear myself talking about Marie, it just comes out, it had to. Marie, slim, as fragile as a reed, *'to be drawn, to be tattooed'* (I exclaim), her dainty breasts, so far only made out beneath her white coat, etc. Dimitri listens, attentive, interested, nodding his head. Asking questions. And where did you meet her and what does she do? When are you going to see each other again? Soon, when I go for the results of my blood test. The pleasure of talking about the woman you love. A pleasure that is supported by your friend, the dependable man who listens, encourages you to confide in him. The love story can begin once it becomes a narrative, a narrative told in the third person that needs a third person, otherwise there's no narrative. Dimitri's ear, his urgings (*and* followed by another inevitable and conventional question) intensify my desire, stimulate my feelings. Marie, yes, Marie's like this, talks like that, dresses in this way… Everything about Marie.

When I'm alone, I look at it. Naked in front of the mirror, I only have eyes for it. It: my *Vulnerant*. It sometimes seems to be in motion, as if it's turning on its axis, the cross starts moving, becomes a wheel, accelerates, the wheel is transformed into a circle, a shape devoid of writing. Could my *Vulnerant* be a helix driven by its own energy? When the helix stops revolving, I come to again, I notice a smear of ink, faint but visible, where the words *Vulnerant omnes* used to be, still that smear, still the words *ultima necat* clearly legible, only the words *ultima necat*. Unashamedly perfect.

Where can the letters and words have gone? Soon the last trace of *Vulnerant omnes* will have disappeared. Its total disappearance will be a shock. Get used to the idea. I persuade myself that this tattoo cut in half, amputated, will be as beautiful as it was in its original form. The half-sentence being sufficiently aesthetic in its meaning and colouring. But am I really convinced?

To leave some trace. The great obsession of human beings. Myself above all. How can we bear the idea that nothing of ourselves survives? How can we contemplate our ephemeral nature without getting dizzy? Having the tattoo done was a response to that malaise, an ineffective response since it will disappear *post mortem*, when the body decomposes, but at least its not as ephemeral as *built-in obsolescence*. That much-talked-about built-in obsolescence you find everywhere nowadays, not only in consumer goods but also in human relationships. It's the very definition of fashion, a phenomenon that is spreading more and more and shaping our attitudes, making us hysterical, superficial, restless, unsettled.

Marion

I've never got married. Never wanted to, never could, I don't know. If I do have any children, I'm not their father, that's not the appropriate word, *progenitor* would be better, or why not *donor* as they have in sperm banks? I've always been fascinated by the idea of sperm banks, I've amused myself renaming these worthy institutes: 'Masturbation brothels', 'Slop-pails for future generations', 'Our sperm is neither weak nor lazy, we check it, we choose it', 'Mothers-to-be R Us' etc. However, I do hope I've made a mark on women. I like to think so, when I'm old I'll imagine some unknown progeny, faceless offspring ejected from the wombs of my lovers as if their conception was the work of the Holy Ghost. Free for good from the responsibilities of being a father, I nonetheless secretly hope to have been behind the birth of numerous innocents. I will add that satisfaction to my conviction that I was an unforgettable lover for my exes. How could some of them ever forget me? I think of Marion.

At the time Marion is 22, I'm 17. I remember her fondly, with a touch of nostalgia. We're young. I'm inexperienced. Not for long.

She's a secretary at the *lycée*. She's just started, immediately after having completed her qualification. In her appearance she outshines all the girls at the school. The boys there have registered this pretty blonde who's scarcely older than them and is different from the other girls because she's free of the dross of adolescence that causes greasy skin, makes them chubby and pustular, puffy and ashamed of it. They're taken with her old-fashioned charm, her reserve. Any old excuse is good enough for the guys in my class to go to her office. It's who can get the smile, the glance, the *double entendre* that the others would have liked to enjoy. I desire Marion. Doubtless because my classmates would like to lay her down in the grass and make her groan, doubtless as a challenge, doubtless also because she's *truly* irresistible. I show her my drawings (a pregnant woman, naked, with her hands round her stomach, a Dantean staircase linking heaven and hell, done in Indian ink). I can already draw very well. I play the melancholy artist. Marion, impressionable, is aroused. I can sense it. One day, as she's seeing me to the door of her office – we're talking about Goya, she's very cultured – I seize the occasion. I go up to her, take her hands, draw her to me. She hesitates, blinks, looks alarmed then compliant and what I wanted happens with the speed of a car accident. Just the speed, not the violence. Her moist lips and the sigh I'll never forget, the sound of a bird in distress.

It's the year I'm doing my baccalaureate. I don't spend a lot of time studying but I know enough to get through the exam.

The summer holidays, sunshine, no commitments. I have Marion to myself. And, finally, the grass the boys were dreaming about and Marion groaning in my ear, her passionate outpourings addressed to *me*. And something of *The Devil in the Flesh*.

In July we meet every day. I leave her at the beginning of August for a young persons' summer camp during which I learn to handle a canoe. A holiday camp which allows me to cut a figure with my virgin fellow campers by explaining the details of the *ars amatoria* to them. They hang on my lips.

Marion calls me when I get back. She's pregnant. We arrange to meet.

— You never told me you weren't on the pill.
— Was it too much for you to consider it, to ask me?
— I was just an innocent boy, I didn't realise.
— If I didn't feel like crying, I wouldn't be able to stop laughing.
— What's going to happen now?
— What do you think's going to happen?
— I'm going to the Beaux Arts, I'm not ready to…
— I'd assumed that would be the case. I'll manage.

The new academic year starts in October. And for me it is indeed to be the prestigious École des Beaux Arts in Paris. The architecture of the place impresses me as much as its high-flown name. I've become someone, a student artist, a romantic young man who leaves home in the morning with a portfolio of drawings under his arm, dresses in black, lights his fag with pretentious gestures. The future belongs to me, Art is calling, I'm a genius beneath the cupolas, in the glass-roofed Palais des Études and the lecture theatres; one day my talent will be recognised; I will be rich and famous. I rent a room in one of the student residences, my parents can't help me very much financially and after a few months I'm stony broke. My savings are swallowed up by the drawing materials that have to be regularly replenished and then there are the student evenings where you spend money on drink and partying: you drink, you wear yourself out, you squander your own time and your parents' money.

I never ring Marion again, never see her again. I don't even think of her any more, concentrating as I am on my studies, on making a success of them or, rather, on my new life and the parties. Later on I can't help feeling a vague sense of pride at the idea of having got a girl pregnant. It gives me a feeling of virility I sometimes boast about when, gossiping with my friends after a few glasses, I feel important and behave accordingly. I boast about it, strutting like a cock, with the relish of a young man starting out in life with petty triumphs.

Then suddenly, after all these years, I feel the need to see if I can find some trace of Marion. If I've ever been attached to a woman and if something of that union remains, then that woman can only be Marion.

The online telephone directory, Facebook, Twitter etc. I click on the link. Has she changed her job? Is she married? All at once the questions are piling up, while before there was – nothing. Marion C. (Now how did she spell her surname?)

I find a trace, her surname coupled with another, doubtless her husband's. Joy. Directory enquiries gives me a number. My thoughts gather, the images roll past. Twenty-eight years ago, it makes my head swim. As I say 'twenty-eight' I'm seized with horror. The child's age. A child who is now a man. I could run into him in a bar, in a public lavatory. Perhaps I have come across him *already*? I imagine the scene: the conventional smile one has for any stranger, the 'have you got a light?' and the little grin that goes with it. The terrible banality of coincidence. Palpitations, a cold sweat. The trace, what trace did I want to leave? That of a living being I left behind me, abandoned. I could be discouraged but in fact my impatience becomes more acute. The telephone before me turns into an object of desire and of hatred. I can't take my eyes off it. The object becomes a means of getting into her house by surprise, as effective as breaking and entering. Ring up Marion? What for? I just want to know, I think, in order to reassure myself.

Answerphone (a male voice says 'we will ring you back'). I explain quickly. I hang up with a vague feeling that I hope no one will return my call. What an idiot I've been. What is Marion to me, or the little boy or girl person we conceived in the aberrations of our youth, especially mine.

Three hours later it's *her* voice on the telephone. I've no idea who you are, Marion says. Stunned, struck dumb, I'm tempted to hang up at once. I repeat my name. No, I'm sorry, I *really* have no idea.

But you are Marion C? I ask with a hint of reproach in my voice that she must surely hear.

Oh yes, just a minute, yes, she eventually says. Drawing hope from her final word, I ask about the child. He's doing well, Marion says, thank you for asking.

Oh, the turmoil in my chest! Breath held and released, a warm throb running through my veins, surging up from my chest again, spreading through my brain, an effervescence of joy, a pyrotechnical frenzy, a shower of breathtaking wonder. Thirteen, Marion goes on. He's just had his thirteenth birthday. (The number 13 appears in large figures.)

Blazes of light like shards of glass right in my eyes. Visions. I see before I understand. The child is not mine.

How did you know I have a son? Marion asks in a gentle voice that I spontaneously qualify as *maternal*. And the next moment requalify as *terrible*.

You don't remember? You were, well, you know…

I was what?

She's starting to sound tart. She's getting annoyed, she's wasting her time, she has nothing to say to me, she's no idea what I'm *getting at*. More exasperated than nasty. A maternal *exasperation* that has a *terrible* effect on me.

It leaves me agape, my mind in a whirl. After a moment I stammer, uttering the words the way you spit out for one last time: No, no, it doesn't matter. I thank her and hang up.

I wipe my forehead, I'm bathed in sweat. I've got a temperature again.

Traces

Impossible not to feel shattered after this encounter with an episode from my past. As if I'd really been waiting all those years for news of that child and had suddenly become aware that the wait had been a sham, a huge lie I'd been living with.

I ought to have been unconcerned about it, viewed it as a lot of hassle about leaving traces. But without them, what is there left of oneself? Someone once asked: Where does the white go when the snow melts? A man leaving no memories, a traveller with no luggage, type making no impression… someone who's left nothing behind him verges on the pathetic, dragging his despair along behind him to the four corners of the earth. Doubt, invasive, saps his strength; the years pass, he meets people, organises his life, perhaps creates some works and nothing remains. The summing-up recalls his years learning the catechism, *For dust thou art, and unto dust thou shalt return.* He thinks of the desert, of the immensity he has crossed many a time without understanding, of the calm constituting his existence despite the superficial clamour of petty events he lives through without conviction. The shadow following his body has suddenly grown smaller, soon all that is left will be a dribble of thought, an archaic perception of his existence, the sole idea he will have of himself. That is to say: nothing.

At my age especially the idea of simply disappearing *without leaving any trace* is intimidating. Some men get married for less than that. Comfort and strength found in another person, procreation. Duplication of oneself, multiplication of responsibilities, extra difficulties to give one a stronger existence, prospects. Why not me? I've nothing against it in principle. Have I waited too long? I can't remember ever having had the opportunity. I must have missed out on one of life's major events.

I piece together Marie's face from my memories, exhausting myself with frustration. See her again, I absolutely have to see her again. Even if only to put an end to the mental construction work around her. See her to stop thinking about her.

I'm convinced that everything would be different with her, at last an explosion of meaning in this great void. You meet someone, you embrace their first name and it establishes itself inside you.

The day when I go back for the results of my blood test is one of excitement and delight. The possibility of seeing Marie again. Happy, nervous, apprehensive – but the fear I feel has nothing to do with the possibility of an illness in my blood. The fear is entirely devoted to Marie.

I couldn't care less about the diagnosis, no one could care less about it than me. The lab's a local health centre that only employs a few nurses. I get there early. Perhaps I'll see her going to work, in a hurry, her hair still damp from the shower.

Some young women open the metal shutters, come and go. Five minutes later they can be seen in their white coats. There's something saintly about this profession, these young women should proceed to the holy sacraments, distribute hosts. It would comfort patients, help them get better more quickly. The people are waiting in a line, well-disciplined, we're behaving like a priest's flock. No Marie on the horizon. I wait, I let people go before me. It's futile. The lab assistants bustle about, they've been at the centre since it opened, the staff are all there. Roles distributed between those who deal with the paperwork and those who pierce veins, between those who celebrate the office and those carrying out menial tasks.

I won't see Marie today. I wasn't going to bother about my diagnosis. In my disappointment the results of my blood test seem immaterial. My lymphocyte count is abnormally high. I shrug my shoulders. So what? I'm not worried, not afraid, just hugely indifferent. It's a bit like walking round in a foreign country, you leave your worst troubles behind you, that's the whole point of the trip. I'm advised to see a doctor as soon as possible. What's all the fuss? I look all round. There's a more serious matter: the absence of Marie.

That night I can't sleep, I keep tossing and turning. Palpitations. My heart's a schizophrenic marathon runner approaching its built-in obsolescence date. As long as it only stops after it's reached the finish. And the finish will be the next time I see her.

The disease begins with an 'L'. The doctor advises me not to live through this time alone. I ought to talk to someone. I remain silent. Who could I tell about this illness the doctor's trying to explain and that remains nonexistent for me? I don't feel ill, at least *not really* ill. I tell the doctor this. His look is full of kindness, no, commiseration. He says, 'The treatment consists of an injection of interferon every…' He repeats what he's just said. It seems to me. I'm not listening any more. His mouth forms an 'o', presumably he's asking me a question. I visualise the verb *to interfere*: I interfere, you interfere, we interfere. We observe each other, he with a nice smile. Then he asks whether I've got any family or friends. I reply in the affirmative, thinking of Claudio and Marilisa, Dimitri. Why trouble my Italian friends with these worries. Isn't Dimitri my family? We're a family of two: him and me. It's all I've got left.

I will keep Dimitri informed. I make the promise looking the man straight in the eye; he wouldn't have let me leave his surgery without it.

Back in my flat I start drawing again in a fairly relaxed way. Even without the itching I can feel where I have my tattoo, my body's causing me no problems.

In front of the mirror. Only the words *ultima necat* appear, the rest has disappeared as if by magic, as if obliteratd by a laser beam, the dark colour that used to be there will have been reabsorbed into the tissue. What is left of what I called my *Vulnerant*? *They all wound* is no more, all that remains is *the last one kills*.

So *the last one kills* will be the disease, I imagine as I muse. I repeat the sentence before going to sleep, it lulls me to sleep. I don't feel afraid at all.

Contrary to what I told the doctor, I haven't said anything to anyone about it. Not to Claudio and Marilisa, nor to Dimitri. It simply didn't occur to me. I've been living together with the name of the disease that begins with 'L', not with the thing itself. The word went round and round inside my head while I was asleep, which was the reason why I dreamt not of the pathology itself but of the sounds contained in the word: *look* and *mere*. The possibilities of language lodged in our subconscious. A man is looking at a mere. Why doesn't matter, it's the beauty of the phrase: *look – a – mere*. Mere suggests a rural landscape, back to nature, age-old reality unspoilt by the modern world. It reminds me of a picture: a man on a hill is watching another letting his horse drink at a pool while some country folk are loading a cart; there are three cows on the skyline. It's Constable's *Hampstead Heath, Branch Hill Pond.* That shows how a blood sample can take us back to the land. How the abstract can become concrete, the invisible be transformed into the visible. Listen to words.

I go back to the laboratory to see Marie. I go in, I ask one of her colleagues. Marie? She addresses the question to one of the other young women in white coats. Who gives me an odd look. They share a knowing smile. Reply: Marie's coming back from holiday tomorrow. So I'll come back tomorrow. And who is it asking after her? She won't remember me, I say turning to leave. I hear them stifling a laugh, at least that's what I sense, suspect, suppose, as I go out of the door. All at once the blood rushes to my face. The blood they claim is diseased but which is making my face burn as can happen to anyone, to a child caught being naughty, to an adolescent feeling humiliated, a woman who's been slapped. Shame. All that blood as warm and enduring, as red as that which spurts out of the bull killed by the *torero*. Thick blood, scarlet, a viscous liquid that covers crime scenes for a long time. The same blood. My face on fire because of the women's laughter, for their laughter hurts more than that of the children at the swimming pool who were laughing at my tattoo. I feel vulnerable.

One ought to always be wary of epigrams. The same goes for assertions and declarations. Beware of their power. Why did I say, *She won't remember me*? If I hadn't said, *She won't remember me*, Marie would doubtless have remembered me. All in all, my own fault.

When she comes out of the lab, at the time when the white coats are back in their lockers, Marie walks past without seeing me. I wish her a good evening, like any common skirt-chaser, her look expresses annoyance and weariness (oh, not another one, she's thinking). I'd stake my life she doesn't recognise me.

You don't recognise me?

Skin and Ink

Here I would like to digress for a moment: there are ways of addressing another person which automatically make you likely to win or lose. Some people arouse the negative reaction they imagine they fear but secretly hope for. They present an image of themselves that is so weak and pathetic that their real intentions are the opposite of what they maintain. They wallow in a sort of failure in order to gratify a lachrymose disposition. A success or a triumph would do nothing for them, they make sure that never comes about; they're cowardly, defeatist and no one in the whole wide world can understand them. They doubtless hate the whole wide world anyway. They look as if they're saying, 'I'm still a little baby who still throws tantrums and wants to inconvenience the whole world because he's unhappy and wants that to be known.' A possible parallel with a beaten wife who reminds her torturer husband that she's got a back, arms, a face ready to receive his blows. The woman groans, irritating the man and knowing that she's irritating him. (Sadomasochistic couples a possibility?) Snivelling is not inoffensive. I've always hated this attitude in others, though I have to admit that it's a tendency that's not entirely unknown to me. I find it quite difficult not to give way to this inclination, just as you scratch a sore even though you know it's wrong. It's not a frame of mind one would call 'virile' in the noble sense of the word and people who're always listening to themselves and secretly feeling sorry for themselves are not real men. But it's not easy to fight such a tendency even when you're aware of its terrible extent. Self-indulgence has its pleasures. There you have my sin, what I call my *tragic flaw*.

As it happens, in this case I forget not to put on a martyred look.

She turns her head to look at me a second time. She's wearing a green macintosh, exactly the same colour as the trees in the street. Doubtless a kind of camouflage – to confuse the male predators who would wait for her when she left work. After a few seconds thinking about it and frowning Marie exclaims: Of course! You're the new doctor, the new member of the lab staff. I'm very much taken with this idea, I almost feel like not contradicting her. She's funny. I stammer. That's not you? It was just that your face seemed familiar…

No, you're right, that's not me, I came for a blood test.

She smiles.

Oh, of course. You must excuse me now, I'm in a hurry.

That's what the beginnings of love look like. Like a misunderstanding. Like a woman quickly taking her leave in a little green macintosh. With a forced smile.

How good it is to assume the role of the romantic hero. I immediately adopt that posture of a man of the nineteenth century. And of course I love the colour green, a colour you find in the paintings of Constable and Caspar David Friedrich. A colour you find on macintoshes. Marie's already a dozen yards ahead of me when I decide to follow her. I'm reminded of Circe's *eternal rustling trail* that Pierre Loti talks about and I add the colour green to the adjective *rustling*. I'm following the wake of the woman slipping away from me in the colour of foliage. I follow her down the street, on the *métro* until she gets home. She doesn't notice me. I am admirably discreet in the way I go about it.

You don't need a code to get into her block of flats. She crosses a courtyard, disappears into another building. From the courtyard I see the light go on in a second-floor flat. I know where she lives. I leave, I will return.

Dimitri takes the discretion of friendship to the extreme of not asking me the results of my blood tests. I love him for that. I am touched that my friend should understand the likes and loathings of a solitary male without my having to explain them to him. He doesn't question me but at that moment he's all attention. His way of coming up to me, of taking my wrist – I'm reminded of the greeting between Roman legionaries who grasped each other's forearm, a practice between men among themselves – the pressure of his right hand and the way he looks me straight in the eye, as if to say, 'I'm here for you.' It makes me feel intimidated, grateful. I smile. Together we agree on a new series of drawings that will become tattoos. A theme: *dynamism*. To be expressed in the elements (fire, water etc) or animals. A few ideas come to me.

He's sat down at his work table, cleared a little space, taken a piece of paper and started doodling. He's absorbed in drawing, sweeping strokes of the pencil, it's a large design, probably a sailing ship or a wave breaking, difficult to tell from where I am. He keeps on talking while he's drawing, his eyes concentrating on the sheet of paper, his eyelids busy.

— Any news of Marie?

— No.

— Not seen her again?

— No.

Does he sense I'm lying? He remains silent. Suddenly:

— You wouldn't like another tattoo?

— You definitely don't like being a one-off tattooist.

Dimitri grins.

— It depends, it all depends, I can assure you.

He throws his pencil down on the table. It must be a sign. End of conversation. Is he annoyed? Offended? Touchy certainly.

On the way home that evening I feel itchy in the place where the words are on my chest. I run my fingers, my nails over it. It's irritated, it's inflamed. I'm bleeding. All at once there's this desire to tear off the skin of that part, that lousy part, dirty part, that problematic spot. I've undone my shirt out in the street. I'm scratching away at my chest like a madman. It's dark, no one notices my strange behaviour and this solitude goes to my head like a spiked drink. Hurry home to check. To check the state of my *Vulnerant* and of my abused skin.

Back home I take off my shirt with such violence the buttons get torn off. I dash into the bathroom, lean my sweat-soaked brow to within a couple of centimetres of the mirror. My face is blurred. I can *see* (my reflection in the mirror) but I *can't see my eyes*. The mirror is a black pool absorbing the details of my body, freezing them in a kind of fright. Everything's inert, and deaf, and – is it the sweat mixed with the fear? – oozing. The walls are oozing, the mirror I'm looking at is sweating like skin, my body's covered in thousands of tiny drops that a fantastic acuity of vision allows me to observe as if under a microscope. Still clinging on to the sides of the washbasin, I lean my chest back. I start. The cross is there! The cross is watching me. It could speak, suddenly animated, eloquent. At that moment I manage to read the first words: *Vulnerant omnes*. It can't be, no, that's impossible. *Vulnerant omnes* had disappeared. I stare at the apparition, incredulous, close my eyes. *If only, if only,* I say to myself. I open my eyes. *Vulnerant omnes* isn't there any more. The magic didn't work, the first words did really fade, I would have simply loved it if… no, that's not being realistic. The skin around is all red but the blood's dried. Still some residues of torn skin under my fingernails, though.

In the street I come across a guy whose face tells me something. I hesitate, I go through my mind. I'm gripped by a sort of panic. I've just seen his forearm. I've recognised his tattoo, it's one of my designs. A distinctive picture of a hunting scene: a horse bolting, nostrils wide with fear, hounds with their fangs bared, eyes bulging, hunting down a stag that is stumbling, one leg broken. A little picture done on ten centimetres of skin. Without wanting to boast, it's one of the marvels in Indian ink I did two years ago. Commissioned by Dimitri. His commission, my execution.

So it wasn't his face that called out to me but the tattoo on his arm, that I must have seen without realising. Generally very shy, I feel a rush of boldness, I go towards him, I hail him. *Monsieur*! Excuse me, *monsieur*!

The guy turns round. I point at the hunting scene.

— I just love your tattoo. Could you tell me the address of the studio where you had it done?

— If you like. It's not far.

— Are you happy with it?

He hesitates before replying.

— In aesthetic terms it's successful, certainly. (He pauses for a moment.) But I'm not going to have any more done.

— Oh, really. Why?

— This tattoo's taking up too much space in my life. It's stupid, I know, but since I had it done I haven't been able to stop thinking about it.

— Because you were so happy with it?

— Not just that. It's difficult to explain and you'll think me stupid…

— Not at all. Do go on.

— Well, I had strange sensations. I was convinced I was being bitten by dogs. It was all inside my head, of course, but back then I found it disturbing. As if the drawing had turned against me. There was nothing wrong with me, of course. I know it sounds stupid…

— No, not at all. But have you had any problems since then, I mean different ones?

— Nothing special. Apart from the fact that I seem to be running into the tattooist a little too often.

— I assume you live in the same district.

— Nevertheless. And then… I shouldn't be telling you this but… And then, after all, this guy, this Dimitri's an oddball.

— I don't follow. Is it the tattooist you're talking about?

— Yes. I hardly knew him but from one day to the next he's become the friend of several of my acquaintances. He appears to be a seductive type. A *seducer* might be the more appropriate expression.

I start to feel uncomfortable and break off our conversation. As I make my way home, I think about Marie again. I get the shivers. Why did Dimitri ask me so many questions about her?

Casus belli

My dread of finding a rival in Dimitri is quickly compounded by my concern at losing a friend. But I refuse to believe that will happen, I'm convinced the tie of friendship is by its very nature indestructible. Faith in him and no need to have faith in her. Anyway, she's not his type. Just as he's not her type. It's impossible. And the next moment: the possible becomes probable, the probable certain. Night. Sweating, palpitations and the multitude of questions-and-answers refuted, accepted, refuted again. I close my eyes and I can see them together as clearly as I can see my own body, my own uneasy body scrutinised in the light of my suspicion. If only I could get rid of these… Put an end to these thoughts, these horribly sharp-focused imaginings. Have done with friendship and love, go on to something else. If only I could manage *not* to see them together. It's too much of an effort for me. Condemned to remain here, I see them down there, Marie's silhouette passing across the closed curtains. The view from the courtyard is as instructive as the view down into the courtyard; you could set so many scenes for crime films there. I wait for night to fall, I don't really know what I expect, I turn over in my bed, the scene I *saw* comes to life in a double setting, up here and down there. I'll see the reason why my attention has been aroused when the moment comes. I make myself as unobtrusive as possible, curled up in the sheets; sticky with my sweat, they feel like strangers. Silent and on the alert, I listen to the sounds inside my head: Circe's *eternal rustling trail*. I hear the sounds associated with Marie, a sound of foliage, a feminine quivering. People go in and out. I don't attract attention. I slip into the shadows, crouch in the darkness where the rubbish bins are kept which is no longer the darkness of my bedroom. And I'm right: after some time, an eternity, a man crosses the courtyard and goes into the block where Marie lives. I hold my breath. A few minutes later it's no longer one but two silhouettes that can be seen behind Marie's curtains. I know that man, that walk, that body, that face. Dimitri.

The lightness of a spirit moving on a breath of air, the lightness of a floating demon. I float over the tangled bodies. What follows is like a scene from a crime film, except that the victim is willing. The male solidity of the torturer gives him control over the woman who yields before him. Convulsive movements. Wings outspread, Dimitri swoops down on Marie. Naked and moving, the man's flabby body is trembling. His tattoos stretch, human and animal figures meet, do battle in silence. The China Sea covers Marie's chest while the dragons attack her thighs. Their claws slash her, their predators' jaws close round the soft parts of the young woman who, half torn to pieces by the voracity of the monsters, half burnt by the fire coming out of their raging nostrils, is screaming as loud as the man in the iron collar, the one stuck for ever on her lover's left arm. There's nothing better to listen to. There's nothing more terrifying. Except that suddenly it's not her any more, it's him who's… absorbing me and terrifying me… That can't be right but it is… I can see it clearly… Something is taking shape on his torso, that I hadn't seen before. A male torso and yet a torso with breasts. For those fatty excrescences are surely *breasts* even though they don't have that function and the superfluousness of their growth is emphasised by the black stars tattooed all round them. The androgyny of a fat man. I get up, staggering. And I repeat to myself, *the last one kills*.

While I used to be the one who phoned him, the one who went to see him, the one making demands, I don't get in touch with Dimitri again. Seen Dimitri too much, watched Dimitri too much, thought about Dimitri too much. I knew the guy, knew him alone it seems to me, but in a way that suited me by dreaming about him, by giving his image substance. A fine lie for a devious character. I created this man in accordance with my wishes. No, I created him in accordance with his own lie, his fine appearance. I wanted him to be like that, splendid and reliable, and I find that… The telephone rings. It's him. I can't remember what I was saying. He wants to see me. Claims to be impatient, to be looking forward to seeing me. What now? What should I do? There's a faint crackling on the line. Why should I see someone who's not worthy of my trust? It just came out. Without my realising. A long silence like breathing behind the crackling on the line. Dimitri goes on:

— Have I done something wrong? Am I not your friend any more?

— I think you've been hiding things from me.

— What things?

— Your attraction to the woman I've just met and whom I've fallen in love with.

— My God!… Oh no, not that, not that again.

— What d'you mean 'not that', 'not that again'?

— Listen. I'm very much afraid you're going through something similar to what a couple of my previous clients have experienced.

— And what would that be?

— Some people had the impression that I was getting involved in their lives after I'd tattooed them. One claimed I was following them everywhere. Another thought I'd taken the flat next to theirs in order to keep an eye on them. One man even thought that…

— That?

— That I'd seduced his fiancée.

— And that wasn't the case?

— From your tone of voice I suspect you're convinced it was the opposite.

— You're not going to answer my question?

— Well, no, I had no intention of stealing his 'property'. But as chance, *chance*, I say, would have it, I was terribly attracted to the young woman and the attraction was mutual.

— I don't understand.

— I didn't know she was engaged to him. People don't introduce those close to them to me before I tattoo them.

—You're interested in Marie. It's no use denying it, you were asking me hundreds of questions about her.

— How immature you can be sometimes. I'm interested in the people you go round with. As a friend.

We say goodbye to each other. There was no declaration of war between us. But on my side a suspicion that hasn't healed over. A feeling I don't approve of but can't do much about.

Performatives

'In certain cases making an utterance consists neither in writing what one is doing nor in asserting it, but in doing it. That is what is called the theory of performatives.' (An article on performative art in *Chroniques culturelles*.)

To write is to do.

TRIGGER OFF THE ACTION.

Does Dimitri know that he turns his clients' lives upside down by tattooing them? Or has he made a decision not to know? One way or the other he must be aware of his gift. He knows that he doesn't disappear from the lives of those he's tattooed just like that. He's intoxicated by it because it assures him that he has power over other people. And he has nothing against exercising it in an underhand manner. It shields him from suspicion, from people settling the score. His art is not simply a representation or a stylistic device, it's the word in the biblical sense, the Word with a capital W. The realisation of his will. Of his Will with a capital W as well. Tattooing becomes a performative art, the tattooer in action creates reality. It's the beginning of an assault that's at once psychological, real and symbolic. Dimitri can employ his gift with absolute impunity. So far no one has dared to call him to account for his actions, since no one has an inkling of his performance. But I have, I've understood. His performance is a tour de force. He becomes involved in the lives of those who have been under his hands. He is the demiurge artist who interferes with the lives of his clients who become his creatures. With their skin, with their innermost self.

Writing *Vulnerant omnes, ultima necat* on someone's skin is to tie the future of the man with the tattoo to the meaning of the words, it is to determine his fate. In my dream Dimitri has breasts, Dimitri sleeps with Marie, the woman I love. In the *ultima necat* scenario the last one is not Marie, even though the Latin word is feminine, as it is in French. It's Dimitri. Dimitri the destroying angel who is fiendishly both man and woman. Woman. *Elle*.

That's assuming this *elle* is not of a different kind. What can be hiding behind that blasted feminine pronoun?

Elle is 'L'. The disease beginning with 'L', polluting my blood. My organism is intimately acquainted with the female circulating inside me without asking permission of anyone. Attacking the corpuscles, responsible for my tiredness, my dizzy spells. Exploiting me. And if I do nothing, 'she' will kill me. My blood discoloured, the red gradually fading, a progressively transparent fluid. All the medical handbooks say that 'she' will kill me if nothing's done. And I can well believe the medical handbooks.

I've bought the drugs, put them on my bedside table. I haven't opened the packet. It's there waiting. We look at each other.

Soon it will be the fashion *not* to have a tattoo, which will have become the rarest thing in the world. Imagine virgin skin. As immaculate as at birth. As pure as clear water. People will exclaim: Oh, you've no tattoos! How marvellous! That is right, isn't it? You're not hiding one in some intimate place? Isn't it splendid, all that unsullied skin, even beauty spots hardly catch the eye. You never tire of admiring that pristine expanse. And what a pleasure it is to lift up your hand to touch that virgin continent. To embrace it with no image to check your impulse, to distract your attention. A discovery that recalls the enthusiasm with which people venture out into the wide-open spaces: the Australian interior, the Rocky Mountains or the watery expanse of the ocean.

But it will be a long time before that day arrives. In reality it's not even close. How long will we have to put up with seeing hideous designs on innocent human skin that has not asked for anything. And worst all is the range of this vulgar fashion. People are never short of imagination when it's a matter of being vulgar, it's an area where they are very creative. Visual puns, obscene pictures, botched drawings. The navel orifice used as a cat's anus; a sketch of a couple locked in coitus with two arrows, one pointing to 'your mother' (for her the position on all fours), the other to 'me' (the active partner behind). The tongue, the skin of the genitals impregnated with ink. Dog turds, corpses, vampires with red eyes, alsatians, a copy of the original bow-wow. The more you see, the more flabbergasted you are. And why not someone's name, as in the days when cattle were branded with the owner's initials? Wait for people to lift up their clothes. Their fantasies shine forth on pot bellies and dimpled backs. And why not have a tattoo of a little chap whose hair could be one of the tufts you have on your own body? You don't believe me? You're wrong.

On whose skin will one see a Chinese dragon and a sophisticated geisha that come gracefully to life with every movement of the muscles and yet apparently independent of them? And the slender figures of Polynesian tattoos, so beautiful they give the body an excess of being, a shamanic force, will they too disappear, taking with them the soul of the skin? In tattooing stupid fashions and jokey trends develop like viruses. But if those who deck themselves out in them are happy with them… Whether they are or they aren't, it's a marriage for life. They will be there for good unless, for want of glass paper, those who can't bear them any longer treat themselves to sessions under the laser. Following which a scar will appear, a souvenir as durable as what it replaced. THE SCAR IS EVERLASTING.

It's Dimitri who's just turned down the side street, I'm sure (almost sure). The other day I was sitting in the bus and I saw him on the terrace of a café. He was reading the paper. His head was bent down but that didn't stop me recognising him even if what I mainly saw was his bald-shaven-shiny skull, his big hands and his rings, a bit too showy for a man. And his way of tilting his head slightly to one side. His broad shoulders sticking out on either side of the newspaper. It can only have been him. And now he's crossing my path again. How many more times? I'm not mistaken, I know for sure. Who else could have that bearing? The bearing of a well-built man with a paradoxical feminine side that makes him bend in a strange way, makes him supple from inside – from duplicity? He's the one I draw in the illustrations I do for magazines. He's the one I see when I think about Marie. I can't think about Marie any more without Dimitri's silhouette disturbing my reverie. A reverie that will remain a reverie, nothing more. I haven't had the courage to go back and try to pick her up. I'm firmly convinced Dimitri would come between us. He would be there at our rendezvous before me, he would be the first to take her in his arms. He would be there before me in order to inspire unbridled passion deep within her womb. He would be the one to reply yes yes to her loving question-pleas and his hands, his amber- and silver-ringed hands, would calm, would arouse the incredible need that makes Marie's skin quiver.

I think of Dimitri as of the name of Demeter. Demeter, the goddess of fertility, taught men the art of making wheat grow on earth. Dimitri limits himself to skin. He produces tattoos for lack of wheat. But our skin is everything. The earth of humans is our skin.

THE CURSE IS EVERLASTING. In certain cultures writing is a sacred art, the spirits are invoked by the written word. Writing is dangerous, its powers mobilise invisible forces, call out to the dead wandering through the night listening to the incantations of the living. The magic power of words lasts until what carries them disappears. If the words had been put down on parchment, the parchment would have to be destroyed for the spell to cease. Acts of violence alone can overcome what is sacred.

Marion was an exceptional young woman: she didn't read the usual books for her generation and it was on her advice that I read Bernanos. *Mouchette*, a short tale, the story of a young girl from an impoverished family who, having been seduced by a tramp whom she sees as a redeemer, heads straight for disaster and chooses suicide. At one point she has to look after her mother, who is ill. The story is set in the Ardennes at the beginning of the twentieth century, people are cold, they die of hunger. Mouchette uses flour and warm water to make poultices to relieve her mother's pain. In taking care of her mother she is depriving herself of food (the flour is the only thing left to eat in the house). Recalling the story of Mouchette suddenly cheers me up. Why? I'm convinced I can see the way out of my own distress in this story. The poultices, the plasters made of flour applied to the chest.

There's no doubt that Marion taught me everything. Ungrateful, like many young men, I didn't recognise her generosity in both human and cultural terms, her good influence on me. But you have to be able to acknowledge your own mistakes. Marion was to be a shooting star in my life. Radiant and transient. Transient because of me, because of my juvenile superficiality… I must go back to Mouchette after all these years. Must read *Mouchette* again. I kept the copy Marion lent me in my library. A rush of nostalgia at the sight of the yellowing pages. Reading this book again brings back memories. But not just that. A plan takes shape. There's only one way of escaping from this curse. The curse of my *Vulnerant*.

As in the theory of performatives, the tattooing sets off the action, in this case the disease beginning with 'L'. The tattoo predicted that it, the last hour, will kill; *Vulnerant* has seen to it that it, the predatory female, the disease, is going to kill. *Vulnerant* – a performative tattoo. Remove the tattoo. What other possibility is there? The mere thought of the liberation fills me with joy. Why hadn't I thought of it sooner, I mean given it *serious* thought? I reread the passage in which Mouchette smears the mixture of flour and water over her mother's stomach. Then she licks her fingers (she's starving) and the mixture tastes like cake to her. And her mother has to be saved with this paste like a second skin.

Isolate the tattoo. Mark out the zone. Purify myself with the help of a poultice. It's midnight. I'm alone in my flat. The city is asleep. I know there's some flour left in the kitchen. I occasionally do some cooking. I light a fag. I've always used those Zippo lighters that you have to refill with petrol regularly. I examine the Zippo refill. A little metal cylinder. Half full.

More than enough. After having savoured the cigarette, that I refuse to think of as my *last one*, I take off my shirt. Bare -chested, I pick up the packet of flour, take out a handful, it feels like sand – childhood memories. I pour the petrol onto the little white pile and knead. The fat in the hydrocarbons produces lumps. Little whitish balls that I press together between my palms. Slowly working on this medical dough, I think of the baker's work, its sensual mythology. For centuries kneading dough has been a hallowed act. A ceremony. I have formed a slightly sticky ball that my hands continue to knead. The ball becomes a cylinder and then is flattened, becomes a ball once more, as dense as a minuscule planet. I breathe deeply, feel calm. I've always felt composed when it was necessary to proceed serenely. The awareness of the importance of what is at stake. The day I took my baccalaureate I remembered absolutely everything from my courses without having been a conscientious pupil. The image the mirror sends back to me is that of a robust man, still young, and I'm grateful for that. *Vulnerant* stands out from my skin like a helix with one blade broken. In the oblique lighting of the bathroom part of my body remains in the shadow, my head, my legs are swallowed up in the darkness. Strange relief: my extremities have left me and it doesn't hurt. Very, very gently I apply the paste to the tattoo, following its shape, taking great pains. Thus the original design is returned to me. Regular and luminous – of an almost unreal whiteness – it's really striking. I stare at it for a good while, enthralled, as is only right, by its (re-) appearance. What a good idea it was, this mark in the form of a cross. How obvious. Nothing ever disappears entirely and forever, things that fade away can return. Everything was there, waiting on or under my skin. Everything was in me.

I've had enough of you, *Vulnerant*. I don't want you any

longer. It's time you left me in peace. You've told me your truth. You've repeated it often enough. Your curse is on its last legs. I have decided to have the last word myself. All empires come to an end and the harsher their rule, the more spectacular their fall. Don't you dare try appealing to my better nature. What mercy did you show me? It was a joy to have you on me, yes, that pleasure, that choice did exist, but only briefly – for how long, two or three weeks? – then suddenly it was gone. I've got over you. I'd tired of your presence well before you started uttering curses. That's what happens with tattoos, it appears, the satisfaction they give only lasts for a brief moment, then people either regret having had them done or they don't see them any more – so what's the point, why all this *parading the skin*?

The smell of flour mixed with petrol is filling my nostrils suggesting an accident at a baker's or a cake-frenzy at a petrol station. The mixture is warming my skin. The dermis is going red under the white paste, I can feel it. *Vulnerant* is watching me in the mirror. It's alive, it's come back to life, it's regained strength, the plaster has regenerated it. It wants to skin me alive.

Someone once said, we're all free, if only we knew. Do you hear that, *Vulnerant*? I'm free. Unconditionally and without you. My reflection vanishes from the mirror and when it reappears there's something in my hand. There's an object in my hand that makes me laugh. White teeth in the mirror. I flick the little spark wheel on the Zippo. Everything goes ahead as expected. The hideous mouth of a dragon snaps up the flame. A dazzling flash. For the fraction of a second I see the burning crosses of the Klu Klux Klan, then the pain comes to erase all memory.

I'm saved! I'm saved! I'm saved!

The author would like to thank the tattoo artists who answered her questions:

Yann Dowork
Heloïse Guay de Bellisen
Rudy Oddity

Dedalus Euro Shorts

Dedalus Euro Shorts is a series of short European fiction which can be read from cover to cover on a Eurostar journey or on a short flight.

Titles available:

Helena	Ayesta	£6.99
My Little Husband	Bruckner	£7.99
An Afternoon with Rock Hudson	Deambrosis	£6.99
Ink in the Blood	Hochet	£7.99
Alice, the Sausage	Jabès	£6.99
Lobster	Lecasble	£6.99
Las Adventures des Inspector Cabillot	Marani	£6.99
The Staff Room	Orths	£6.99
On the Run	Prinz	£7.99

Forthcoming in 2016:

The Prodigious Physician	Sena	£7.99

These books can be bought from your local bookshop or online from your favourite internet retailer. For further details of the Dedalus list please go to our website www.dedalusbooks.com or write to us at Dedalus Limited, 24–26 St Judith's Lane, Sawtry, Cambs, PE28 5XE for a catalogue.

Lobster – Guillaume Lecasble

'There was a Lobster-shaped hole in world literature which has now been filled by this remarkable work.'

Nick Lezard's Paperback of the Week in *The Guardian.*

'The surrealist tale of a lobster on board the Titanic which finds itself helplessly attracted to a human female, the book hinges on the life-changing orgasm the fishy amorist gives Angelina as the boat sinks in the icy water.'

Tom Fleming in *The Literary Review*

'This weird and wonderful little fable is like the awful offspring of Hans Christian Andersen and Salvador Dali: it is filthy romanticism and heart-breaking smut.'

S.B. Kelly in *Scotland on Sunday*

'A fable of crustacean love. Our hero is a lobster aboard the Titanic. From his tank, he watches his father being eaten by a pretty girl. Then the boat founders and Lobster escapes. Aboard the sinking ship, Angelina, the girl who ate his dad, knows a brief but shattering moment of physical love with Lobster. Then they are separated. They pine for each other. Angelina tries having sex with another lobster, with disastrous results. Death smells of bay leaves.'

Sam Leith in *The Daily Telegraph*

'Ludicrous and macabre, as well as erotic, this is some kind of tour de force.' Ray Olson in *Booklist*

£6.99 ISBN 978 1 903517 34 5 110p B. Format

Alice, the Sausage – Sophie Jabès

'This surreal frenzy of melancholy and black humour is a fable concerning the fragility of a female self-image that is continually shaped by society. A flippant criticism from her father leads Alice to subjugate herself to varying degrees of humiliation in an effort to please all around her, as she becomes a vessel for food and sex. The resulting grotesque denouement involving cannibalism and twins escaped from a mental hospital is barely digestible.'

Dave Thomas in *Buzz Magazine*

'Experiencing sex for the first time, her need for answers grew more unruly and her sexual encounters more frequent. However her appetite was still insatiable. Alice grows in size until her exquisite body is no longer recognisable. This euro short story is dark and sickeningly twisted and will definitely make you think twice about ever over-eating.'

H. Forbes in *The Crack*

'Alice goes round Rome adoring herself until her father tells her she is not pretty and must therefore be "nice to men". So immediately she starts eating and eating, swelling up into a slumped mess unable to leave the house, while pleasuring any random man in return for food. This is lovingly described and Alice's speciality is eating at the same time as being "nice".'

Scotland on Sunday

£6.99 ISBN 978 1903517 51 2 120p B. Format

Staff Room – Markus Orths

'Dedalus has made an important contribution to British culture by publishing European fiction in translation. They love writers who deal in what they call distorted reality – the unusual, bizarre and surreal – such as this wonderful satire, translated from German by Mike Mitchell, which is as funny as it is savage.' David Sinclair in *Tribune*

'The English translation of German writer Orths' darkly humorous satire about a teacher trying to stop a nightmarish totalitarian regime damaging the school system is a hit in the author's homeland. This translation by Mike Mitchell retains Orths' absurdity and penchant for the ridiculous.'

Alex Donohue in *The Big Issue*

'Absurd, hyperbolic, paranoid, and funny – *The Staff Room* tells the story of Kranich, a newly qualified secondary school teacher's experience at his first job. Curiously, the students rarely figure in the tale. The story focuses on the administration, namely the headmaster, and his illogical, "Big Brother-ish" attitude towards employees. Kranich suffers through the headmaster's and the broader school system's inane rules and petty priorities. Meanwhile, his more seasoned colleagues get by whinging at pubs and avoiding work. Kranich feels alienated and lonely, unable to find reliable support anywhere.'

The Crack

£6.99 ISBN 978 1 903517 55 0 102p B. Format

Las Adventures des Inspector Cabillot – Diego Marani

Inspector Cabillot, the first Europanto detective tackles varied European concerns such as a mad cow disease terrorist cell that takes over London and the kidnapping of a major European Union leader by Finnish nationalists who want to replace Europanto with Finnish as the only language of the European Union. These stories take a light-hearted look at the European Union and its problems in a language created to give Europeans a common tongue.

'Marani's ability to see humour in his longing for a universal language has flowered in his creation of Europanto, a jovial, pan-European tongue which began in his office and spread to columns in Swiss and other newspapers, some of which have been collected in *Las Adventures des Inspector Cabillot*. The book does not need to be translated: Europanto is "der jazz des linguas. Keine study necessite, just improviste, und tu shal siempre fluente esse in diese most amusante lingua". Take a framework of English word order, varied with the occasional German inversion, and chuck in whatever vocabulary occurs to you from French, German, Italian and occasionally Latin… Pretending to anarchy but addicted to rules, Europanto is a paradoxical creation. In the comic mode of *Las Adventures des Inspector Cabillot* the contradictions jangle merrily.'

Matthew Reynolds in *The London Review of Books*

£6.99 ISBN 978 1 907650 59 8 138p B. Format

The Prodigious Physician – Jorge de Sena

This astonishingly erotic and ironic novel is set in vaguely medieval times, but the tone is starkly modern.

A young gentleman is travelling on horseback from somewhere to somewhere else, and stops by a river to rest and bathe. The Devil arrives and (almost) has his way with him. The young man resignedly accepts this because, when he was still a beardless youth, his godmother had sold his soul to the Devil in exchange for extraordinary magical powers, which are invested, it seems, in a special cap he wears.

As he is lying there naked after bathing, three maidens appear and, trying to avert their gaze from the young man's many charms, they tell him the story of their recently widowed mistress, who is dying of grief. None of the usual physicians can help her. She can only be saved by a man who fulfils three conditions. Since he more or less fulfils these conditions, the young man duly goes to the castle. Despite the scoffing protests of the local priest, he saves the queen, who immediately falls in love with her saviour.

But are the maidens and the queen what they seem? Is the prodigious physician what he seems or is he a devil? In this novel, nothing is certain and nothing is ever entirely over, but returns again and again.

£7.99 22 April 2016 ISBN 978 1 910213 38 4 140p
B. Format